For Siân
P.B.

Orchard Books
96 Leonard Street, London EC2A 4XD
Orchard Books Australia
Unit 31/56 O'Riordan Street, Alexandria, NSW 2015
The text was first published in Great Britain in the form
of a gift collection called *The Orchard Book of Fairy Tales*,
illustrated by Ian Beck, in 1992
This edition published in 2001
First paperback publication in 2002
Text © Rose Impey 1992
Illustrations © Peter Bailey 2001
The rights of Rose Impey to be identified as the author
and Peter Bailey to be identified as the illustrator have
been asserted by them in accordance with the
Copyright, Designs and Patents Act, 1988.
A CIP catalogue record for this book is available from the British Library
ISBN 1 84121 572 4 (hardback)
ISBN 1 84121 580 5 (paperback)
1 2 3 4 5 6 7 8 9 10 (hardback)
1 2 3 4 5 6 7 8 9 10 (paperback)
Printed in Great Britain

Jack and the Beanstalk
and
The Three Wishes

Retold by Rose Impey
Illustrated by Peter Bailey

ORCHARD BOOKS

Jack and the Beanstalk

There was once a poor widow who had nothing in the world but a son called Jack and a cow called Milky-White. Jack was no help. He was a dreamer; he couldn't keep a job for two days together. But Milky-White was a good milking cow and saved them both from starving. However, the time came when the cow grew too old and her milk dried up. Then there was trouble.

"Now we're ruined," said the poor widow.

"I'll get a job, mother," said Jack.

"We've tried *that* before," said his mother. "No, there's nothing left but to sell the cow."

"Leave it to me," said Jack. "I'm just the lad to strike a bargain." And the same day he set off for market.

Well, Jack hadn't gone very far
when he met a little old man, and
couldn't he talk!

"Good morning, good morning and
what a morning for a bargain. You
look a smart lad," said he. "Where are
you going with that fine cow?"

"To market," said Jack.

"I might be able to save you the
trip," said the man.

This news pleased Jack; he was
already feeling weary.

"And because I like the look of you and that *handsome* cow," said the little old man, "I'm going to give you such a bargain. What do you think of these?" And he held out his fist, opened his fingers, and there in his palm were five...beans.

"Beans?" said Jack.

"Beans!" said the man. "Not just one bean, not two beans, not even three nor four," said the man, "but five beans is the bargain and you won't get a better one."

"Five beans for my cow? You must think I'm daft," said Jack.

"These aren't any old beans," said the fast-talking man. "Believe me, these are magic beans. Plant them overnight and by morning they'll have grown into a beanstalk that'll make a hole in the sky."

Well, the word magic caught Jack's imagination. He took a closer look at the beans. They shimmered like a rainbow. They looked magic, all right.

"It's a deal," he said, and he pocketed the beans, handed over the cow and was home before his mother had finished her work.

"Back already?" she said, amazed. "I hope you got a good price."

"You'll never believe it, Mother," said Jack, bursting with excitement.

"Oh, Jack," she said with relief. "How much did you get? Ten pounds? Fifteen? Surely not twenty?"

"Better than that, Mother," said he. And he opened his hand with a flourish and showed her the five beans. His mother was speechless. But not for long.

"Beans!" she yelled. "Beans? You sold my pride and joy for a handful of beans? You idiot. You fool. You nincompoop!"

Jack's mother snatched the beans out of Jack's hand and threw them through the open door. "That's what I think of your precious beans. Up to bed with you. There'll be no supper tonight. Or any other night from now on." And she sat in the kitchen and wept with temper and hunger combined.

Jack climbed the stairs, a sad and hungry boy, but more sorry for his mother than his own empty stomach.

Next morning when Jack woke he wondered where on earth he was. The little window which usually let in the morning sun cast a green glow over the room, as if it were under the sea. Jack slipped out of bed and across to the window. Outside an enormous beanstalk twisted and twined its way into the sky, breaking through the clouds, its stalk as thick as the trunk of a full-grown tree.

Clearly, Jack had been right to
trust the beans, and he didn't hesitate
now. He reached out into the branches,
pulled himself up and disappeared
among the dense leaves.

Jack climbed and he climbed and
he climbed for most of the day until,
utterly exhausted, he reached the top
of the beanstalk. There was nothing in

sight but a wide, winding road. Jack walked along the road until at last he came to a huge great house, and at the door of the huge great house was a huge great woman.

"Good morning," said Jack, nice and polite. "I'm almost dead from hunger. Please, could you give me a mouthful of something?"

"It's a mouthful you want is it? It's a mouthful you'll *be* if my husband catches you," said the huge great woman. "He's an ogre. He eats boys like you on toast."

"I'll just have to take my chance," said Jack. "I'm dead anyway if I don't have something to eat. You wouldn't want that on your conscience, would you?" And Jack gave her the kind of smile that would charm any ogre's wife.

"Oh, all right," said she. "But be sharp. He could be back any time." She led Jack into the kitchen and gave him a bowl of porridge.

But as soon as he started to eat, the bowl, the table, the whole kitchen began to shake.

"Quick, here he comes now. Into the oven with you. And not a sound or it'll be toasted boy sandwich and no mistake."

Before he could object, the ogre's wife had bundled Jack into the oven, leaving the door open the tiniest crack.

The shuddering came closer and closer.

Thump! Thump! Thump! Thump!

Jack heard a voice like thunder
booming down the tunnel:

"*Fee-fi-fo-fum,*
I smell the blood of an Englishman.
Be he alive, or be he dead,
I'll grind his bones to make my bread."

The ogre thumped the table. "Where
is he, Wife?"

"There's no one here," said she.
"That's leftovers you can smell – last
night's stew. Come and eat your
breakfast."

Jack and the Beanstalk

and

The Three Wishes

For Siân
P.B.

Orchard Books
96 Leonard Street, London EC2A 4XD
Orchard Books Australia
Unit 31/56 O'Riordan Street, Alexandria, NSW 2015
The text was first published in Great Britain in the form
of a gift collection called *The Orchard Book of Fairy Tales*,
illustrated by Ian Beck, in 1992
This edition published in 2001
First paperback publication in 2002
Text © Rose Impey 1992
Illustrations © Peter Bailey 2001
The rights of Rose Impey to be identified as the author
and Peter Bailey to be identified as the illustrator have
been asserted by them in accordance with the
Copyright, Designs and Patents Act, 1988.
A CIP catalogue record for this book is available from the British Library
ISBN 1 84121 572 4 (hardback)
ISBN 1 84121 580 5 (paperback)
1 2 3 4 5 6 7 8 9 10 (hardback)
1 2 3 4 5 6 7 8 9 10 (paperback)
Printed in Great Britain

Jack and the Beanstalk
and
The Three Wishes

Retold by Rose Impey
Illustrated by Peter Bailey

ORCHARD BOOKS

Jack and the Beanstalk

There was once a poor widow who had nothing in the world but a son called Jack and a cow called Milky-White. Jack was no help. He was a dreamer; he couldn't keep a job for two days together. But Milky-White was a good milking cow and saved them both from starving. However, the time came when the cow grew too old and her milk dried up. Then there was trouble.

"Now we're ruined," said the poor widow.

"I'll get a job, mother," said Jack.

"We've tried *that* before," said his mother. "No, there's nothing left but to sell the cow."

"Leave it to me," said Jack. "I'm just the lad to strike a bargain." And the same day he set off for market.

Well, Jack hadn't gone very far
when he met a little old man, and
couldn't he talk!

"Good morning, good morning and
what a morning for a bargain. You
look a smart lad," said he. "Where are
you going with that fine cow?"

"To market," said Jack.

"I might be able to save you the
trip," said the man.

This news pleased Jack; he was
already feeling weary.

"And because I like the look of you and that *handsome* cow," said the little old man, "I'm going to give you such a bargain. What do you think of these?" And he held out his fist, opened his fingers, and there in his palm were five...beans.

"Beans?" said Jack.

"Beans!" said the man. "Not just one bean, not two beans, not even three nor four," said the man, "but five beans is the bargain and you won't get a better one."

"Five beans for my cow? You must think I'm daft," said Jack.

7

"These aren't any old beans," said
the fast-talking man. "Believe me, these
are magic beans. Plant them overnight
and by morning they'll have grown into
a beanstalk that'll make
a hole in the sky."

Well, the word
magic caught
Jack's imagination.
He took a closer
look at the beans.
They shimmered
like a rainbow. They
looked magic, all right.
"It's a deal," he said, and
he pocketed the beans, handed over the
cow and was home before his mother
had finished her work.

8

"Back already?" she said, amazed.
"I hope you got a good price."

"You'll never believe it, Mother,"
said Jack, bursting with excitement.

"Oh, Jack," she said with relief.
"How much did you get? Ten pounds?
Fifteen? Surely not twenty?"

"Better than that, Mother," said he.
And he opened his hand with a flourish
and showed her the five beans. His
mother was speechless. But
not for long.

"Beans!" she yelled.
"Beans? You sold my
pride and joy for a
handful of beans?
You idiot. You fool.
You nincompoop!"

Jack's mother snatched the beans out of Jack's hand and threw them through the open door. "That's what I think of your precious beans. Up to bed with you. There'll be no supper tonight. Or any other night from now on." And she sat in the kitchen and wept with temper and hunger combined.

Jack climbed the stairs, a sad and hungry boy, but more sorry for his mother than his own empty stomach.

10

Next morning when Jack woke he wondered where on earth he was. The little window which usually let in the morning sun cast a green glow over the room, as if it were under the sea. Jack slipped out of bed and across to the window. Outside an enormous beanstalk twisted and twined its way into the sky, breaking through the clouds, its stalk as thick as the trunk of a full-grown tree.

Clearly, Jack had been right to trust the beans, and he didn't hesitate now. He reached out into the branches, pulled himself up and disappeared among the dense leaves.

Jack climbed and he climbed and he climbed for most of the day until, utterly exhausted, he reached the top of the beanstalk. There was nothing in

sight but a wide, winding road. Jack walked along the road until at last he came to a huge great house, and at the door of the huge great house was a huge great woman.

"Good morning," said Jack, nice and polite. "I'm almost dead from hunger. Please, could you give me a mouthful of something?"

"It's a mouthful you want is it? It's a mouthful you'll *be* if my husband catches you," said the huge great woman. "He's an ogre. He eats boys like you on toast."

"I'll just have to take my chance," said Jack. "I'm dead anyway if I don't have something to eat. You wouldn't want that on your conscience, would you?" And Jack gave her the kind of smile that would charm any ogre's wife.

"Oh, all right," said she. "But be sharp. He could be back any time." She led Jack into the kitchen and gave him a bowl of porridge.

But as soon as he started to eat, the bowl, the table, the whole kitchen began to shake.

"Quick, here he comes now. Into the oven with you. And not a sound or it'll be toasted boy sandwich and no mistake."

Before he could object, the ogre's wife had bundled Jack into the oven, leaving the door open the tiniest crack.

The shuddering came closer and closer.

Thump! Thump! Thump! Thump!

Jack heard a voice like thunder
booming down the tunnel:

"Fee-fi-fo-fum,
I smell the blood of an Englishman.
Be he alive, or be he dead,
I'll grind his bones to make my bread."

The ogre thumped the table. "Where
is he, Wife?"

"There's no one here," said she.
"That's leftovers you can smell – last
night's stew. Come and eat your
breakfast."

He chopped once, twice, clean through the beanstalk. For a moment it seemed to hang in the sky, then it crashed to the ground, bringing the ogre with it. He fell head first with such force that he was buried to the waist, legs in the air – stone dead. And that was the end of him.

So with more money than they could ever spend and the harp to always keep them happy, Jack and his mother had nothing left to wish for, except for Jack to marry, which in time he did. And then, since three can live as well as two, they all lived together and may still be doing so, for all I know.

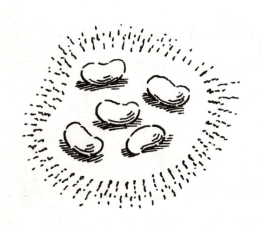

The Three Wishes

One night a man and his wife were sitting before their fire, talking, cosy-like. She was a good wife and he was a good man so they were passing happy, most of the time. But now and again the pair of them couldn't help feeling just a bit envious of their neighbours, who were richer than them.

"It don't seem fair," said the wife.

"It certainly don't," said her husband.

"Now, if I had a wish," said she, "I know just what I'd do with it. Ooh, I'd be happier than all of 'em."

"And me," said the man. "Pity there isn't such a thing as a fairy, right here, this minute."

And suddenly there was, right there, that minute, in their own kitchen. All shining and smiling.

"You can have three wishes," the fairy told them, "but take care, once they're gone, that's it, there'll be no more." And then she disappeared. She was very business-like.

Well, the couple were amazed. They felt as if they had their heads on back to front.

"Whatever d'you make of that?" said he.

"I'll tell you what I make of it," said she. "I know fine well what I'll wish for – not that I'm wishing yet," she said, quick as a flash, in case the fairy was listening, "but, if I *were*, I should want to be handsome, rich and famous."

"Where's the use in that?" said he. "That won't stop you being sick and miserable or dying young. Far better be healthy and hopeful and live to be a hundred."

"And how would that help, if you were poor and hungry in the meantime?" said she. "Just prolonging the misery, in my opinion."

Well, her husband had to agree with that.

"Hmmm," said he. "This is going to need some thinking about. I reckon we'd best go to bed and sleep on it. We'll be wiser in the morning than the evening."

"True enough," said his wife.

But the fire was still burning brightly, so they sat on a little longer, talking things over cosy-like.

They were feeling that happy.

"It'd be a waste to leave this nice fire," said the man.

"It does seem a pity, though," said she, "we've nowt to cook on it. I wish we had a dozen sausages for our supper."

Uh-oh! No sooner said than done.

Down the chimney fell a long chain of sausages and landed at their feet. And that was one wish gone.

The man was flummoxed. He could hardly speak for rage.

"A dozen sausages! What a witless woman is my wife. Of all the harebrained individuals... I wish the dozen sausages were stuck on the end of your nose, you nincompoop."

Uh-oh! No sooner said than done.

The sausages leapt up on the end of the wife's nose and hung there like an elephant's trunk. And that was two wishes gone.

"Oh flipping heck, what have you done to me!" said she. She took hold of the sausages and tried to get them off. She pulled and pummelled them, she twisted and turned them, but they wouldn't budge. In sheer temper she jumped out of her chair, stepped on the end of them and almost tripped up. By now she was fizzing mad!

Her husband sat there open-mouthed, just watching.

"Don't just sit there gawping, you owl, do something, for goodness sake," she cried.

So then the husband tried too. He grabbed hold of the sausages and he pulled and he pulled. It was a regular tug-of-war. But the sausages just stretched longer and longer and longer. When he finally let go they sprang back like a piece of elastic, boxing his wife round the ears – biff! biff! biff! Then they hung down, long and floppy again.

"Oh, what a wretched woman I am," she began to cry. "Whatever will I do?" And her tears ran down the sausages.

"Don't fret," said he. "I know just what to do. We must use our last wish to make ourselves very rich. Then I shall have the smartest gold case in the world made for you to wear over the sausages. Maybe a matching crown. You'll look very grand."

"Are you a complete idiot?" said the wife. "Have you totally lost your senses? D'you suppose I want to spend the rest of my days trailing sausages on the end of my nose? You must have a screw loose. I want the last wish to get rid of these sausages," she said, "or...I shall throw myself out of the window."

And to show she meant it, she rushed across the room, threw open the window and jumped up on the window-sill.

Then her husband couldn't help but smile. The sight of his poor wife, standing on the window-sill with a string of sausages hanging from her nose, was such a comical sight. And, after all, they were still sitting downstairs, so she hardly had far to jump.

But he was a
bit of a tease and
he couldn't resist
winding her up
one last time.

"Of course, my dear, you must do
whatever you think best, but it does seem
a pity, knowing as how you wanted to be
famous and all that. And truly, the more
I look at it, the more it grows on me. I'm
really beginning to think as it suits you."

"Suits me? A nose as long as a
skipping rope? I should be tripping over
it every way I turned," she cried.

"Happen you could wrap it round
your neck, lovely, then it'd serve as a
scarf an' all," he said, trying to be
helpful.

At this, his wife was fit to explode, but the man couldn't keep it up a minute longer. He started to grin, so he got up and helped her off the ledge. For he did truly love her.

"I wish my wife could have her nose back to normal," he said.

Da daa! No sooner said than done.

The sausages fell on the floor and coiled themselves up like a pet snake.

"Well, some good's come of the bad," said she, "at least we still have the sausages."

"I'll build up the fire," said he.

"I'll put on the pan," said she.

"What a good idea," said he.

So that's what they did.

The pair of them sat late into the night, frying sausages and toasting their toes before the fire, and talking, cosy-like.

HANS CHRISTIAN ANDERSEN TALES FROM ORCHARD BOOKS

RETOLD BY ANDREW MATTHEWS
ILLUSTRATED BY PETER BAILEY

Orchard Fairy Tales are available from all good bookshops,
or can be ordered direct from the publisher:
Orchard Books, PO BOX 29, Douglas IM99 1BQ
Credit card orders please telephone 01624 836000
or fax 01624 837033
or e-mail: bookshop@enterprise.net for details.

To order please quote title, author and ISBN
and your full name and address.
Cheques and postal orders should be
made payable to 'Bookpost plc'.
Postage and packing is FREE within the UK
(overseas customers should add £1.00 per book).

Prices an